George Herbert Moberly

The Christians in Rome

George Herbert Moberly

The Christians in Rome

ISBN/EAN: 9783337381882

Printed in Europe, USA, Canada, Australia, Japan

Cover: Foto ©Andreas Hilbeck / pixelio.de

More available books at **www.hansebooks.com**

ARNOLD PRIZE ESSAY, 1861.

THE CHRISTIANS IN ROME,

DURING

THE THREE FIRST CENTURIES.

BY

GEORGE HERBERT MOBERLY, B.A.

SCHOLAR OF CORPUS CHRISTI COLLEGE, OXFORD.

" Victi victoribus leges dederunt." *Seneca.*

OXFORD,

· HENRY HAMMANS;

WHITTAKER AND CO. LONDON.

1861.

THE

CHRISTIANS IN ROME,

DURING THE THREE FIRST CENTURIES.

——

It has been said, that to leave the authority of
Scripture for that of tradition, is like leaving the
summit of a high hill where all is brilliant sun-
shine, and descending its side in the midst of
impenetrable mist.   In the enquiry which is now
proposed, the mist gathers closely round our
steps from the first; we have almost nothing of
the bright sunlight of Scripture to guide us; we
are plunged into sudden darkness at the abrupt
end of the history of the Acts: and it unfolds
itself but gradually and scantily, so as to shew
but little of the features of the landscape for
the first three hundred years.   The very foundation of the Roman Church is a matter of
question.

**FIRST
CENTURY.**
No certain information is given us
in Scripture either of the time *when*, or
of the persons *by whom*, that Church
was founded.   St. Paul writes an Epistle to the
Church at Rome; he tells them that their faith

was already spoken of through the whole world[a]; 'brethren' come to meet him when he is being brought prisoner to Rome[b]: these are the only direct references we have to the subject. It is implied in these expressions, that a Church of unusual strength and vigour had been growing up in Rome, previously to the time at which they were written: but no direct information is given us by Scripture as to its foundation, progress, or extent.

But on one point all, even those who adopt the most opposite theories upon this question, seem to be agreed: that it was through the Jews that Christianity first crept into Rome; through the permission of Jewish rites and customs, that the introduction of Christian rites and customs was tolerated. That there was a large and flourishing colony of Jews at Rome under the early emperors, brought there probably by Pompey after his eastern war, is beyond a doubt. So large was it, that the Transtiberine suburb, a 'monstrous cantle' of the city, was assigned them as a Ghetto[c]—the Jews' quarter. No consistent policy was uniformly pursued with regard to them by the early emperors. Augustus, it seems, favoured them; for Josephus speaks of an embassy of Jews to Rome, which was supported by above 8,000 of the same nation resident there[d]: and the same em-

---

[a] Rom. i. 8.   [b] Acts xxviii. 15.

[c] *Philo*, leg. ad Caium. p. 1014. τὴν πέραν τοῦ Τιβερέως ποτάμου, μεγάλην τῆς Ῥώμης ἀποτομὴν, κατηχομένην πρὸς Ἰουδαίων.

[d] *Josephus*, Antiq xvii. 11.

peror issued a rescript to the Asiatic cities for the protection of the Jews, and the security of their religious worship[c]; which therefore, it would seem, must have been well protected in his capital. But Tiberius drove them from Rome[f], and Caligula ill-treated and insulted them[g]. Nevertheless, the very fact of such ill-treatment leads us to expect an increasingly influential population; "a nation often chastised, yet largely increasing[h]," which are the terms in which Dio Cassius speaks of them. The same writer speaks of their being perfectly free and open in the exercise of their religion in the time of Pompey[i]; and says, that in the time of Claudius they were forbidden by an edict to assemble together, though this was the only one of their peculiar customs which was put down[k]; language which can hardly mean less than that the custom of worshipping openly in synagogues, which had begun in the time of Pompey, was still in use in that of Claudius. His edict may have been the immediate cause of what followed—a tumult, "at the instigation of Chrestus[l]," the result of which was

[c] *Milman's* Early Christianity, vol. ii. p. 25.

[f] *Sueton.* Tib. 36.

[g] *Euseb.* ii. 5, 6.

[h] γένος .... κολουσθὲν μὲν πόλλακις, αὐξηθὲν δὲ ἐπὶ πλεῖστον. *Dio Cass.* xxxvii. 17.

[i] *D. C.* xxxvii. 1.

[k] τῷ δὴ πατρίῳ νόμῳ βίῳ χρωμένους ἐκέλευσε μὴ συναθροίζεσθαι. *D. C.* lx. 6.

[l] Judæos, impulsore Chresto assidue tumultuantes, Româ expulit." *Suet.* Claud. 25.

that the Jews were again banished from Rome.
This took place probably in A.D. 54[m].

By this decree, as is well known, Aquila and
Priscilla were expelled from Rome, and took
refuge, with many others probably, at Corinth,
where they fell in with St. Paul[n], who came
southward to that city just about the same time.
At the end of a year and six months, when they
were left by him at Ephesus as he was sailing to
Antioch, we find them competent to instruct
others more perfectly in the way of God[o]. When
Paul writes his Epistle to the Romans, probably
four years after his arrival at Corinth, he greets
Aquila and Priscilla first among the friends of
whose names his last chapter is full—calls them
"his helpers in Christ Jesus[p]"—salutes "the
church which is in their house[q]:" thus shewing
clearly that they had not kept their light to
themselves.

This then (A.D. 58.) is the first date at which
we have documentary evidence that the Gospel
was taught in Rome; and it seems likely that it
was upon the death of Claudius (which happened
the year before this) that the rigour of the late
edict was relaxed, and that the Jews crept back
to their old quarters. But we do not certainly
know that this was the first date of the introduction of Christianity into Rome. Many are
of opinion that Christians had found their way

[m] *Hemsen's "Paulus,"* p. 405.
[n] Acts xviii. 1, 2.   [o] Acts xviii. 26.
[p] Rom. xvi. 3.   [q] Rom. xvi. 5.

thither long before, and that Aquila and Priscilla were already converted before they met with Paul. Bertholdt even supposes that the Gospel had reached Rome during the lifetime of Christ: others say that the "strangers of Rome," who were present at the great Pentecost[r], must have carried it back to their native country. But this is mere unauthenticated conjecture: the only passage which may possibly be evidence for a prior date is that of Suetonius already quoted,— that the Jews raised a tumult at Rome "at the instigation of Chrestus[s]"; which may be an allegory pointing to a dispute about Christianity which caused the expulsion of the Jews by Claudius.

It is impossible to determine this question with certainty. When we examine the eighteenth chapter of the Acts, to see if it is probable that Aquila and Priscilla should have been already Christians upon their arrival at Corinth, the Sacred text does not help us materially. All we can say is, that it is expressly said to have been "because he was of the same craft[t]," that Paul joined himself to them, not because they were fellow-Christians: and that it is more likely that they should have been two of the Jews whom he "persuaded[u]," than that such an important additional motive for his abiding with them should have been omitted, had it existed. It is clear that, if the Gospel had been taught among the Jews at Rome before this date, it could not have

[r] Acts ii. 10.
[t] Acts xviii. 3.
[s] *Suet.* Cl. 25.
[u] Acts xviii. 4.

been taught by an Apostle, or even by any distinguished convert to Christianity: for Paul, in his Epistle, lays claim to not building "on another man's foundation[v]." On the other hand, if the Roman Church had been proximately founded by himself, that fact would not only explain his use of this expression, but also would be a good reason for his writing to the Romans—the only Epistle extant to a Church he had never yet seen—and expressing such an ardent desire to come among them.

While therefore it must be allowed to be possible that the Church of Rome was founded by Jews at an earlier date than 54, the probability seems to lie the other way. But on whichever side of the question the truth lies, it is clear that it was among the Jews, in the Transtiberine quarter of the city, that Christianity first made its appearance in Rome. The greater number of the Christians would naturally be Jews, but not all: for some Gentiles appear to have been converts from the first. The earliest document which throws light on Christian Rome is Paul's Epistle to the Romans, written the very year after the death of Claudius. This, though it is mainly addressed to Jews, (many of its arguments being such as Gentiles could hardly have understood,) is said at the opening to be addressed to all the saints in Rome[x], Jews and Gentiles; and among the twenty-nine names of persons greeted at the end,

[v] Rom. xv. 20.   [x] Rom. i. 7.

five[y] are derived from the Latin, not from the Greek, and therefore may fairly be assumed to represent Gentile natives. But the proportion of the Jews being so great, we can well understand how Jewish usages and practices came from the first to have a hold over the Roman Church : how it required all St. Paul's most forcible language to make the Jews among the believers cease from despising their Gentile brethren : and how, even after Paul's death, there still should have lingered a party in the Church who *Judaized*, that is, who strove to bring the Church which the Gospel had freed again under the yoke of the Jewish law.

Such was the state of the Church when Paul came to Rome, not as a free visitor, but as a captive. If we remember how small, as yet, was the number of Christians compared with that of the Jews, it will not surprise us to find that the Jews professed ignorance of him and his religion[z], and attended in great numbers a meeting to hear him " expound the kingdom of God" in his hired house, where he was allowed to remain by the kindness of Burrus, the prætorian præfect. In the two years during which he lived there he begot many children in the faith, and those of all ranks ; from those of Cæsar's household to the poor slave Onesimus. But his chief successes were among the army : the fact and the cause of his imprisonment, he himself says, were well known in the

[y] Junia, Urbanus, Rufus, Julia, Lucius.
[z] Acts xxviii. 21, 22.

prætorium [a], a barrack attached to the palace on the Palatine; probably the often-changed soldier, whom the harshness of Burrus's successor caused to be chained to him, belonged to the prætorian guard; and centurions had always been forward in the reception of Christianity. When he is liberated at the end of the two years, we lose sight of him for a time.

His converts may have done much to restore the balance between the Gentile and Jewish portions of the Church. Anyhow, it is probable that they were now more equally proportioned than before: and, it seems, at bitter strife between themselves. It is singular that while the Church has scarcely been founded at Rome, when it must have wanted all its strength to resist those outside, we should find evident traces of two parties in it mutually opposed to each other. But the book which purports to be by Clement, the third bishop of Rome, and which really seems to be the work of some Judaizing Christian in Rome, reveals to us an extent of strife in the infant Church which would hardly have been believed. It is a defence of St. Peter against Paul—of Judaic against Anti-judaic Christianity; and though unnamed, it is at Paul evidently that the writer directs his censure and sarcastic inuendoes all through the work.

The mention of St. Peter leads to another topic of great difficulty: the determining of the measure of his relation with the Roman Church. It is well known, that successive church-historians grow

[a] Phil. i. 13. (with Alford's note.)

in their certainty about his movements, till Jerome in the fourth century assigns twenty-five years for his bishopric of Rome. These accounts, if they stood alone, would not be of much weight, since it is evident that each depends upon and amplifies the accounts of his predecessors ; even Eusebius's testimony must here be received with more caution than usual, as he wrote after Constantine had established Christianity as the religion of the State, when it would obviously be to the credit of Roman ecclesiastical antiquity to have lengthened St. Peter's stay at Rome as much as possible. It is more difficult to go against the consentient testimony of the universal Church, which from all quarters talks of the Roman see as " cathedra Petri," "successorium Petri," as early as the third century. Yet we have every historical probability bearing the other way. We find him still at Jerusalem till after the Council of Jerusalem[b], which is never placed before A.D. 48, and by the best authorities not till A.D. 53. Thus disappear Jerome's twenty-five years. He is not mentioned even for a greeting in St. Paul's Epistle [A.D. 58], which he surely would have been had he been there. After this it is impossible to speak with confidence : but we know that at the Council of Jerusalem his share in the work was agreed to be to go to the circumcision[c]; so it seems strange that he should have selected Rome, the capital of the Gentile world, for his head quarters. His first Epistle contains a greeting from " her of Babylon"

[b] Acts xv. 7.   [c] Gal. ii. 9, 7.

to the Church of Asia[d] : and it seems hardly
straightforward to suppose, with Eusebius, that he
was speaking there metaphorically of Rome as the
great whore of the west: especially as we do read
of great colonies of Jews in Babylonia. It may
be thought, that the existence of a party who said
they were of Peter, proves that he had at least
visited Rome in person: but this it is not necessary
to suppose. There were three parties in like
manner at Corinth when Paul addressed his first
Epistle to the Corinthians,—Petrine, Pauline, and
Apolline[e],—yet no one supposes from this that
Peter had been at Corinth. Rather the mutual
opposition of the Judaizing and Hellenizing
Christians in Rome goes against the supposition
of the presence there at one time of both Peter
and Paul. But all[f] concur in placing his death at
Rome, with that of Paul, in the Neronian persecution; and here there is no adverse testimony.
And we shall understand how Peter, captured at
a distance, should be brought to Rome for con-
demnation and execution, even though he was
no Roman citizen as Paul was, when we read that
this was exactly the case of Ignatius of Smyrna,
also no Roman citizen[g], in the second century.
May not the tradition of the Church, which
represents him as having exercised the episcopal

[d] 1 Pet. v. 13.   [e] 1 Cor. i. 12.

[f] The testimonies to St. Peter's death at Rome are three:
Irenæus adv. Hær.—*Dionysius* of Corinth apud Eusebium—
and *Epiphanius*.

[g] *Blunt's* Three First Centuries, p. 69.

authority in Rome for some years before his death, have arisen from the notorious fact that the Roman Church originally was Jewish ? Peter was the Apostle of the circumcision, known to be especially directing his efforts to the conversion of Jews, and the head as it were of the Jewish portion of the Church ; so that it seems at least possible that the name of " Petrine" may have originally attached to it from this, and been asserted with greater vehemence as the strife grew more angry between this and the Gentile or Pauline party : till in a few generations it was forgotten that Peter had not actually been among the Romans, especially as he suffered and left his bones among them.

The suggestion that the story of Peter's residence at Rome only points to the existence of a Petrine party in the Church, naturally leads to another suggestion. Eusebius says, that Peter, " the great champion of the Apostles," " like God's noble general, wearing God's armour of proof[h]," came to Rome to support the Church against the wiles of Simon the Magician, his old foe. The story of Justin's confirmatory of this, that he had seen an altar to " Simon Sanctus" in Rome, has been sufficiently disproved lately by a discovery in the same spot of an inscription to the Sabine god " Semo Sancus[i]." Notwithstanding this, Simon

---

[h] *Euseb.* ii. 14. τὸν καρτερὸν καὶ μέγαν τῶν ἀποστόλων. οἷά τις γενναῖος Θεοῦ στρατηγὸς, τοῖς θείοις ὅπλοις φραξάμενος.

[i] *Robertson's* Church Hist. vol. i. p. 41. n. *Milman's* Early Christianity, vol. ii. p. 98.

may have been at Rome : but, without judging the story of Eusebius to be mythical, the Roman tradition will be sufficiently accounted for, if we suppose that Orientalism, of which Simon Magus was the popular embodiment, had taken root in Rome before Christianity. The insidious mixture of ORIENTALISM with Christianity, and the struggles of the Church to purify herself from the heresies, which all arose from the East, or at least from the speculative fancies which the East infused into the West, will form a distinct branch of the Church's history during these three centuries : and will be found to exercise an influence upon her position at the present day, at least as important as her long and fierce struggles with the PAGANISM of the old Roman empire, or with the JUDAISM which fought against her from the first, and perhaps, while its opposition lasted, was the bitterest foe of all the three.

For let it be remembered, that besides the Jews who had been converted, and who therefore formed the staple of the Judaizing Christians, there was another body of Jews, the original Jews of Rome : who far outnumbered these others, who would hold no communication with them, but who hated the Church with a hatred probably unparalleled in the religious animosities of the world. Before it reached Europe, the Asiatic Jews had found Christianity growing up amongst them, and had strenuously opposed it : the charge which sealed the fate of Stephen was that he meditated innovations in the Jewish

customs[k]; through all the cities of Asia Minor
the fiercest opponents of the Gospel were Jews,
who were filled with envy, particularly it is probable at seeing many of their own number converted, and who were always the first to resort to
violence. But in Asia the chief cause was wanting
which in Rome embittered the Jews against the
Christians. As at Corinth, Gallio cared not to
distinguish between the two sects of an Eastern
religion, declaring it a matter of words and names
and of the Jewish law[l]; so in Rome, the law
courts looked on Christianity merely as a sect
of Judaism, and could not discriminate between
them, because of their contempt for both. The
peculiar customs of the Christians are ascribed to
Jews by Arrian[m]; Seneca uses language to recount
the spread of Judaism which can hardly be understood of anything but Christianity[n]. Thus the
Jews, who had found themselves and their quarter
to be the first where Christianity effected a lodg-
ment in Rome, were forced to become its most
reluctant protectors. They had nursed a religion
against their will, which they hated; they still

[k] Acts vi. 13, 14.　　　　　　[l] Acts xviii. 12—17.

[m] *Arrian* ii. 9. quoted by *Lipsius*, notes to *Suet.* Claud. 25.
ὅταν τινὰ ἐπαμφοτερίζοντα ἴδωμεν, εἰώθαμεν λέγειν, οὔκ ἐστιν Ἰουδαῖος,
ἀλλ' ὑποκρίνεται· ὅταν δ' ἀναλάβῃ τὸ πάθος τὸ τοῦ βεβαμμένου καὶ
ᾑρημένου, τότε καὶ ἐστὶ τῷ ὄντι καὶ καλεῖται Ἰουδαῖος.

[n] *Seneca*, lib. ' contra superstitiones,' quoted by *Augustine*,
de Civ. Dei, vi. 4. De illis sane Judæis conloquendere, ait
" Cura interim usque eo sceleratissimæ gentis consuetudo
convaluit, ut per omnes jam tenas recepta sit: victi victoribus
leges dedecunt."

hated, but could not avoid screening it. It must have seemed to them a peculiar curse, that the Roman tribunals persisted in confounding with them their bitterest foes, with whom they must constantly have been asserting their diversity. But they could not shake themselves free of the parasite which had grown upon them, and which was soon to tower independently, leaving them barren and withering.

At first, this systematic indifference of the authorities proved a safeguard to the Church; for the Jews, though at times ill-treated, were hardly less despised than the Christians. But by the time of Nero's persecution, we find the position of the two religions remarkably altered. The Christians are marked men: we hear of no ill-treatment of the Jews. Heathen writers so far recognise their separate identity as to say, that a race of people, addicted to the superstition called Christian, were afflicted with unheard of tortures. What was it then which brought Christianity into such distinct prominence, as to make it the mark of a persecution from which the Jews were safe?

This has been a perplexing question to many writers: and some have gone far to seek a theory, which should account for Nero's thus suddenly singling out with such precision the Christians from among the Jews to suffer for their Christianity. Milman[o] conjectures that it was the

[o] *Milman's* Early Christianity, vol. ii p. 36   Latin Christianity, vol. i. p. 26.

gloomy predictions of the Christians concerning the fire of the judgment day which brought them into connnexion with the fire of Rome, and so formed, according to Tacitus, Nero's excuse for the cruelties which he delighted in exercising upon them. Such words, no doubt, may often have been on a Christian's lips, and may have served to fasten suspicion upon him, when all Rome was eagerly and tremblingly inquiring for the incendiary. But there is one fact less uncertain than this, which goes far to establish the cause of the unerringness of Nero's persecution. The Jews, as has been said, hated the Christians bitterly. The vindictive assertion of unconquerable difference on the part of the Jews must have been at least as frequent as the occasions of confusion between the two religions on the part of the Roman government. The Jews must have looked forward with revengeful hope to a time, if it ever were in store for them, when they should have possession of the ear of the authorities, and be enabled to crush the rising Christian community. Such an opportunity was afforded to them now. Poppæa, Nero's mistress, strangely called a pious woman by Josephus, espoused the Jewish cause: Aliturus, a Jew by birth, was a favourite actor of the emperor. It happened that at this time Felix, the procurator of Judæa, had sent bound from Jerusalem to Rome some Jewish priests, upon a trivial charge. Josephus the historian, then a young man of twenty-six, a personal friend of theirs, came to Rome to plead their cause.

He was introduced by Aliturus to Poppæa; and having gained her ear, had gained the emperor's. The priests were dismissed, and Josephus was loaded with presents by Poppæa. From this time, no doubt, the Jews were favoured at court: and hence it should not surprise us to hear of the persecution of the Christians. Hence too vanishes all surprise at the precision with which the Christians were identified: the Jews must have marked their principal opponents long since for vengeance when the day of retribution came; and it seemed to have come at last. The delighted vindictiveness which revelled in the invention of new and horrible torments, may not have been entirely Nero's wanton cruelty[p].

In such a time the heads of the Church—Peter and Paul—could not hope to escape: they suffered together, on the same day, according to the account given in Eusebius[q]. But meanwhile, if the Jews had had the principal share in exciting this persecution, it was their last effort of revenge. Poppæa died while it lasted (A.D. 65.): Nero was killed three years after: and in the year of confusion which followed—which saw four successive emperors on the throne—the Jews were lost sight of; and with them the distinction between Christianity and Judaism, clearly seen while Jews were its exponents, was lost sight of too. Equal contempt was felt for both; and this state of feeling lasted until the destruction of Jerusalem, which not only gave the final blow to the Jews as rivals

[p] *Tacitus*, Annals, xv. 44.   [q] *Euseb.* ii. 25.

to the Christians, by taking away the central point
round which Judaism had rallied : but also trans-
ferred the active hatred, which had been the
portion of the Christians in Nero's reign, to the
Jews. They were taxed severely and insultingly,
and ill-treated in every way at Rome. Nay, we
find that to be a Jew was a subject for persecution; for it was on a charge of impiety, coupled
with Jewish manners, that Flavius Clemens suffered death at the hands of his cousin Domitian,
and that Domitilla his wife was banished[r]. Most
writers have supposed that such a strange accu-
sation can mean nothing but that they were
Christians: but it should be remembered, that
impiety was exactly what would be objected by a
Roman to a devout Jewish proselyte, as well as to
a Christian; and that it was the Jewish nation,
not the Christian religion, which had been all
along the enemies of the Flavian house. Still we
are assured by Dio Cassius that many others suffered, some death, some spoliation[s], on the same
charges: and this may possibly include some
Christians as well as Jews. But when we find
that church-historians reckon this as a second
general persecution, we look in vain for more
instances than this doubtful one of loss of life;
and are forced to think that they enforce the
parallel between the ten persecutions and the ten
plagues of Egypt too strongly. Nothing so general

---

[r] *Dio Cassius*, lxvii. 14. ἔγκλημα ἀθεότητος—ἐς τὰ τῶν Ἰουδαίων
ἤθη ἐξοκέλλοντες.

[s] *Ib.* οἱ μὲν ἀπέθανον, οἱ δὲ τῶν γοῦν οὐσίων ἐστερήθησαν.

c

or so horrible can have happened as under Nero without our having heard something of it, as we hear of that, from profane sources; they themselves allow that it lasted for a very short time[t]; and according to Tertullian, Domitian himself coming to his senses—certainly his successor Nerva[u]—reversed the sentences of banishment, and prohibited all further accusations of Jewish manners.

Thus we see that before the end of the first century, within fifty years after the probable date of the foundation of the Roman Church, one of the three great enemies of the Church is powerless to hurt her. Nero's persecution was a last gigantic effort of the Jews to exterminate Christianity: though they employed for this end the civil arm, over which they had temporary power, just as they were forced to convict our Saviour at a Roman tribunal before they could compass his death. Immediately after this, by a strange reverse, they sink with a change of dynasty from counsellors into outcasts; so that to be under a suspicion of Jewish manners is to be open to insult and persecution. But under neither dynasty was Paganism, as such, fully awakened to grapple with Christianity, as such: Nero persecuted the Christian religion, to please the Jewish nation;

---

[t] *Tertull.* ap. *Euseb.* iii. 20. ἅτε ἔχων τὶ συνέσεως, τάχιστα ἐπαύσατο, ἀνακαλεσάμενος οὓς ἐξηλάκει.

[u] *Dio Cassius,* lxviii. 1. καὶ ὁ Νερούας τούς τε κρινομένους ἐπ᾽ ἀσεβείᾳ ἀφῆκε, καὶ τοὺς φεύγοντας κατήγαγε· τοῖς τε δὴ ἄλλοις οὔτ᾽ ἀσεβείας οὔτ᾽ Ἰουδαϊκοῦ βίου καταιτιᾶσθαί τινας συνεχώρησεν.

Domitian persecuted the Jewish nation, not the Christian religion; though, in the ignorance which all Rome then shared with regard to the distinction between them, one must often have been mistaken for the other.

SECOND CENTURY.
The history of the struggles of the Church with external Judaism is thus over; and now, as they diverged more and more, the distinction between them grew more and more marked, till in A. D. 138, on the occasion of BarCochba's rebellion, the Romans, by the foundation of a new colony Ælia on the site of Jerusalem, and the exclusion of Jews from it while Christians were admitted, forcibly shewed their appreciation of the real difference between them. The time was for ever past when a Jew could be mistaken for a Christian; and though their hatred did not relax, they were never again powerful enough to annoy the Church effectually.

The same event which finally distinguished the two religions, was a crisis which must have shaken Judaism *within* the Church. Would the Jewish Christians follow their nation or their religion? Would they be excluded from Ælia as Jews, or admitted as Christians? The course taken by the Christians of Judæa was the best they could adopt: they elected a Gentile bishop, and returned to Jerusalem, leaving some few dissentients at Pella, now clearly marked as schismatics, under the name of Ebionites. But not only in Judæa, but in all the world, and especially at Rome as the

head-quarters of the Gentiles, must the same
event have shaken the credit of Judaic Christianity. Nevertheless, so closely had Jewish
principles inwound themselves with Christianity,
that they still lingered, and are heard of as dis-
tracting the Church, for nearly a century more.
Their loss of influence is well illustrated by the
history of the controversy on the time of Easter.

It is a question whether Rome ever held the
Judaic or Quartodeciman practice on this point—
that which killed the lamb on the fourteenth day
of Nisan, and celebrated the Paschal supper three
days after, without regard to the day of the week.
This question is involved in that of the foundation
of the Roman Church, already discussed :—if the
Church was planted in Rome by Jews anterior
to A. D. 54, it is probable that they would have
adhered to the customs of their country on this
point as well as on others; but if it was not
founded till after that date, and by immediate
disciples of Paul, he probably would have had
influence enough upon them, even though they
were Jews, to introduce his own, the Gentile or
Antijudaic practice ; of always celebrating the Re-
surrection on the first day of the week, and fasting
for a week before it. Any how, by the time of
Bishop Xystus, (A. D. 120.) the Gentile practice
had obtained at Rome. He and his four suc-
cessors, we are told by Irenæus, did not allow the
Jewish usage within their own Church, yet com-
municated, by sending the Eucharist to and fro,
as freely as before with other Churches which did

allow it[x]. In A.D. 159, Polycarp visited Rome, with the intention, among other things, of persuading Anicetus, the then Bishop, to adopt the practice of the Jews, which had been adopted by the Asiatic Churches, over which he presided. But Anicetus was firm, even against the age and saintliness of Polycarp: and though as a mark of personal respect he allowed him to celebrate the Eucharist in Rome[y], (a highly esteemed honour,) they parted without agreement on this point, though with mutual cordiality. But by A.D. 196, the Judaic party have lost even more ground in Rome. For then Bishop Victor[z], not content with the measures of his predecessors, attempts to break off communion with the Churches which held still the Jewish practice. And though he was forced to desist, from the general outcry of universal Christendom, his conduct well illustrates how sensibly the Judaic party must have declined in importance since the beginning of the century. When this matter is dropped, we hear no more of Judaizing in the Church of Rome.

But the Church was now grappling with another deadly foe—more deadly because even

---

[x] *Euseb.* v. 24. οὔτε αὐτοὶ ἐτήρησαν, οὔτε τοῖς μετ' αὐτῶν ἐπέτρεπον . . . . καὶ οὐδέποτε διὰ τὸ εἶδος τοῦτο ἀπεβλήθησάν τινες, ἀλλ' αὐτοὶ μὴ τηροῦντες οἱ πρὸ σοῦ πρεσβύτεροι τοῖς ἀπὸ τῶν παροικιῶν τηροῦσιν ἔπεμπον εὐχαριστίαν.

[y] *Ib.* καὶ τούτων οὕτως ἐχόντων ἐκοινώνησαν ἑαυτοῖς· καὶ ἐν τῇ ἐκκλησίᾳ παρεχώρησεν ὁ 'Ανίκητος τὴν εὐχαριστίαν τῷ Πολυκάρπῳ, κατ' ἐντροπὴν δηλονότι.

[z] *Ib.* Irenæus writes to beg Victor ὡς μὴ ἀποκόπτοι ὅλας ἐκκλησίας Θεοῦ.

more insidious than Judaism. This has already
been mentioned by the name of ORIENTALISM : a
general name, signifying no single set of opinions,
but including all the developments of that
tendency to speculation which characterized the
Asiatics. But its ramifications, fanciful and innu-
merable as they were, all sprang from one great
primary idea, which was but a revival of the
dualistic doctrines of Zoroaster and the Magians.
The characteristic of all Orientalism was a belief
in two Principles—one the creator of good, one
of evil. Ahriman and Ormuzd in disguise were
the two gods who were preached in Rome even
before the advent of Christianity. For whether
we treat the story of Simon Magus as a myth
or not, it is certain that what under such an
explanation it would import—the infusion into
Rome of Oriental ideas before the importation
thither of the Gospel—is true as a fact. But
Orientalism for some time held aloof from the
Church ; they proselytized side by side with each
other without coming into close contact. Simon
himself, though baptized by Philip[a], can in no
other sense be called a Christian. But in the
second century Christians caught the infection of
these heathen fancies, and the dreamy mutterings
of the East found an echo in the West. At the
same time Orientalism assumed a still more alarming character, from being wrought out with all
the subtle refinements of the Greek language :
and becoming Christianized under the name of

[a] Acts viii. 13.

Gnosticism, exercised a more fatal influence on the Church even than Judaism, after it had in like manner mingled with Christianity. The growth and diffusion of Gnostic heresies belongs altogether to the second century of the Christian era. The two religions had not commingled at all before this period; and after it, though heresies traceable to Eastern sources still prevailed, they had departed from the primary idea which originally characterized Orientalism.

Phrygia, immemorially remarkable for religious frenzy, had given birth to two opposite phases of mind—one sternly practical and ascetic, the other wildly imaginative, according to the varying disposition of individuals. These two streams from the Phrygian mountains inundated the whole of the East, and even penetrated westward. Both Marcion and Valentinus, having spread their heresies through Asia, came naturally to Rome as to the head quarters of Christianity in the West; and there was something so singularly taking in their fancies to minds which were at once refined and unpractical, that they were enabled to do much damage to the cause of truth in Rome.

What they had in common may be told in a few words. They both attempted to harmonize the fundamental truths of the Gospel with the Dualism which had been the faith of their country. They both tried to reconcile the Bible language about the One Supreme God, with what was told them of the two Principles by Zoroaster:

an attempt essentially impossible, and therefore a failure. According to Marcion, the creator of matter rivalled, according to Valentinus he was subordinate to, the creator of mind.

Marcion (who, though he gave his name to a sect, was preceded in his opinions by Cerdon[b]) held that there had primarily existed two distinct Principles[c], a good and an evil, the evil Principle being the opponent but the inferior of the good. But this inferiority was practically of so little weight, that the Principles were always at war with one another. This idea he developed in his book called the "Antitheses," where the evil and the good—the Old Testament and the New— the Jews and the Christians—are paired off in mutual opposition.

But *Valentinus* his contemporary solved the problem another way. The Demiurgus, or creator of matter, was no longer the opponent but the descendant of the Supreme God, through a wild genealogy[d]. There was no rivalry here, but complete subordination. The imperfect because material creation of the Demiurgus, was perfected by Christ, also the offspring of the Supreme; the New Testament did not destroy but superseded the Old; Judaism was the childhood, Christianity the manhood, of the world. So while Marcion cut out the whole of the Old Testament to suit

[b] *Euseb.* iv. 10, 11.

[c] *Rhodon*, ap. *Euseb.* v. 13. ἕτεροι δὲ, καθὼς καὶ αὐτὸς ὁ ναύτης Μαρκίων, δύο ἀρχὰς εἰσηγοῦνται.

[d] ' Adv. omn. Hær.' c. v.

his doctrines, Valentinus adopted it entire, assigned it the second place in his system, and accommodated his doctrines to it, though often violently allegorizing its plain meaning[e].

But while these two leaders taught thus the two most easily recognizable extremes of Gnostic opinion in Rome, a third, *Florinus*[f], timidly lifted up his voice with another solution of the problem of the existence of good and evil. There is but one God, he said, but he is the active creator, not merely the passive permitter, of evil, in the same sense in which he is the creator of good. His friend Irenæus—whom we shall see again in the character of a mediator—wrote him an urgent epistle " on Monarchy—or that God is not the creator of evil[g]." The result was the opposite of what Irenæus intended. Florinus wavered: but instead of submitting to the Catholic faith, he at length adopted the views of Valentinus[h], to which (if his alternative lay between the two heresiarchs) his own were evidently more akin; for he was not prepared to admit the two hostile principles of Marcion.

[e] *Tertull.* ' de præscr. hær.' " *Marcion* exerte et palam machærâ non stylo usus est, quoniam ad materiam suam cædem Scripturarum confecit. *Valentinus* autem pepercit: quoniam non ad materiam Scripturas, sed materiam ad Scripturas excogitavit, et tamen plus abstulit et plus adjecit."

[f] *Euseb.* v. 15.

[g] *Euseb.* v. 20. περὶ μοναρχίας ἢ περὶ τοῦ μὴ εἶναι τὸν Θεὸν ποιητὴν κακῶν.

[h] *Euseb.* v. 10. ὑποσυρόμενον τῇ κατὰ Οὐαλεντῖνου πλάνῃ. See *Massuetus*, quoted in *Routh's* ' Script. Eccl.' vol. i. p. 35.

The two extreme Gnostic heresies continued to attract disciples after the disappearance of their first preachers: and they would probably have had more success in their proselytism, had it not been that the speculative tone of the East was becoming absorbed in the practical genius of the Roman world. This practical turn of mind was what really gave birth in the last half of the second century to *Montanism.* Waiving theoretical questions on the origin of evil, and so not recognised as a Gnostic, Montanus was yet an Oriental. He came from Phrygia: religious frenzy worked upon his practical mind, and resulted in asceticism; and his sect, which soon reached Rome though without its founder, was rigorously self-denying. He was an eclectic in his principles: or rather, his sect imitated Marcion in severe discipline, and improved upon the doctrines of Valentinus as to the development of the world, holding Montanism to be the manhood and perfection of mankind, of which Judaism and Christianity were but imperfect stages. As to the moral tone of their mind, the Montanists were the Jesuits of the ancients: exhibiting the same rigorous sternness, the same lofty devotion, the same boldness in proselytism. These characteristics captivated many: and they had been careful, as they hoped, not to incur the charge of heresy by doctrine or discipline opposed to that of the Church; though it is difficult to see how they could have reconciled this pretence with their acknowledged depreciation of the Gospel in comparison with certain pretended revelations of the Holy Spirit to Montanus. But Irenæus—again a peacemaker, "in nature, as well as in name[i]," according to Eusebius—actually came to Rome on an embassy from the Gallic Churches to plead their cause[k]; and bitter were their complaints when the report of one Praxeas of their evil deeds in the east induced the Bishop of Rome to condemn their heresy and excommunicate its leaders[l]. They found a refuge in Africa, which, placed morally as well as locally midway between the East and the West—between the regions of soaring fancies and of hard realities —was a more congenial soil for them; and here it was that they made a convert of the greatest ecclesiastical writer of the time, Tertullian.

Thus before the end of the second century, Gnosticism in both its forms had died out of sight, and Montanism had been formally expelled from Rome. But it is hardly possible to over-estimate the amount of influence which these heresies had upon the Roman Church, while they were flourishing there. The spirit of speculation must have thoroughly infected the whole Church; and it could hardly have been possible for any Christian to hold nakedly the truths once delivered to the

---

[i] *Euseb.* v. 24. φερώνυμός τις ὢν τῇ προσηγορίᾳ αὐτῷ τε τῷ τρόπῳ εἰρηνοποιός.

[k] *Euseb.* v. 4.

[l] *Tertull.* adv. Prax. c. 1. "Nam idem tum episcopum Romanum agnoscentem jam prophetias Montani, &c. et ex ea agnitem pacem ecclesiis Asiæ et Phrygiæ inferentur .... coegit et literas pacis revocare jam emissas, et a proposito recipiendorum charismatum concessam."

saints, without some taint of the new mystical opinions.

But meanwhile that which was destined to be the most powerful antagonist to Christianity was stirring itself reluctantly to the contest. PAGANISM was to be its last and its longest foe, and to play the most conspicuous part among the enemies of the Church. We cannot sufficiently admire the Providence which restrained this most deadly foe for so long, and caused it not even yet for awhile to be fully awake to the destruction which Christianity was to bring upon it. Three circumstances are especially to be noted as having contributed to defer the contest with Paganism, and so to rear the infant Church till it was strong enough to meet that contest.

The first of these has already been pointed out in detail, and need here be alluded to only in summary. It is the way in which Christianity, while in extreme infancy, grew without attracting the notice of Paganism, till it had taken such firm root in Rome, that the utmost efforts failed to eradicate it. We have seen how it grew under the shadow of Judaism, which though cordially hating it, and even persecuting it when it had the power, yet could not avoid unwillingly protecting it. Nero's persecution, as has been already suggested, though commonly attributed to the emperor's wantonness, (never to any deeper cause,) may probably have been caused by Jewish hatred, as it began and ended with the beginning and ending of Jewish influence. And Nero's persecution stands alone, as an isolated fact, in the history of the first century: (for the second so-called persecution was directed more against Jews than against Christians;) so that Christianity had not yet in the first hundred years been weighed on its own merits by Paganism. But by the second century it began to attract more consistent notice: as Judaism grew weaker, and as Christians grew more numerous and influential, it was inevitable that they should force themselves more and more on the notice of the popular religion.

Another circumstance which tended much to strengthen the cause of Christianity was that now, when the tenets of its professors were just beginning to attract notice, the empire had passed into the hands of mild and equitable rulers. Had Nero or Domitian been revived in Trajan and Hadrian, the whole Christian population might have been swept from within the boundaries of Roman rule. But the moderate character of all the four emperors who succeeded Domitian was in favour of the growth of Christianity. It was not that they were too much occupied to weigh the religious state of the empire. Trajan's wars and Hadrian's peaceful policy yet left them time to consider and legislate exactly for the position of the empire in regard to the Church. It was their own moderation which made the wide differ-ence to Christianity between their rule, and that of those who both preceded and followed them; that imperial moderation which culminated in the reign of the wise and benevolent Antoninus. Aurelius, who succeeded him and closed the century, was a differently-constituted man ; equally well-intentioned, and even more earnest-minded, but philosophic and intolerant : and his reign was a bloody period for the Church.

And a third point which tended to moderate the rancour with which Christianity was received by the Roman world was, that Paganism had changed and still was changing *its own* character. Had Christianity in its infancy had to cope with the degrading Polytheism which formed the whole religious belief of the earlier Romans, it would have had to pass through a terrible ordeal indeed, from which there is no saying how far it would have come out victorious. The religion of the Romans at this time was far from being identical with that of their fathers. The deeper thought of the later Greeks had shaken the Roman belief in the many gods, and all was tending to make them centralize, so to speak, their religious faith. The Epicureans, though they admitted the existence of Gods, represented them as idle, and exalted Natural Law into their Supreme Deity : the Stoics boldly rejected the exoteric fables about a plurality of Gods, and declared that there was but One. All the Schools agreed in this—that it was necessary to suppose that One Power governed the universe—call it Nature, or the Unknown God, or whatever else they would. This belief had worked its way through the upper portion, and now was powerfully leavening the mass of Roman society. The old superstitions were kept up in form, it is true; but rather from a politic design of keeping the people quiet, than because all who professed them were satisfied with the popular belief. At the end of the century we find an emperor himself learning and teaching the Stoical doctrines, and no mean expositor of the tenets of Zeno.

Accordingly the dealings which Paganism had with Christianity were at first comparatively mild. Even at the beginning of the second century trials on account of profession of Christianity were rare. Pliny, in his celebrated letter to Trajan, (A.D. 104.) confesses that he had never been present at such a trial[m]: though he had filled the offices of tribunus militum, of quæstor Cæsaris, of prætor, and of consul; and had been proprætor of Pontica for eight or nine years. Thus, though his expression shews that such trials were not unprecedented, they could not at any rate have been common. And we find that when Ignatius is being conveyed to Rome as a prisoner, he seeks to avert the kindly interference of the Roman Christians on his behalf[n]; which shews a spirit of fairness on the part of the government, and disposition to accept Christian evidence, such as we should not have expected in the second century.

---

[m] *Plin.* lib. x. 97. " Cognitionibus de Christianis interfui nunquam."

[n] *Ign. ad Rom.* i. 4. φοβοῦμαι γὰρ τὴν ὑμῶν ἀγαπὴν, μὴ αὐτή με ἀδικήσῃ .... παρακαλῶ ὑμᾶς, μὴ εὔνοια ἄκαιρος γένησθέ μοι.

Such was the disposition of the heathen to the Christians at first, and as long as their religion remained unaggressive. And till it rose to something like a level with the old religion, it must have remained perfectly unaggressive. Who could have been so harmless and innocent in their lives, who could have been such good citizens, soldiers or servants, as devout Christians? The heathen must have been astonished, because they were unaware of their inner principle of consistency, at the sight of a body of men growing up among them unaccountably, so perfectly unaggressive, yet holding to the distinctive points which shewed their difference of religion with such tenacity. They would try at first by persuasion, by remonstrance, by cajolery, to win them to conformity with the common practice; and it would not be till all these milder arts had failed, that they would be driven to more open and violent measures to force them to abjure their faith.

What first no doubt caused the Christians to be noticed was their own rigid (though often timid) abstinence from all participation in the religious rites of their country. The consciences of the first believers, we know, scrupled to partake of meat bought in the shambles, knowing that it might have been consecrated to an idol's service°. Their language would be rigidly and markedly free from all the defilements of pagan oaths. How could they enter the temples of those who were to them no gods but devils? How could

° 1 Cor. viii.

they sanction by their presence the games at
which human blood was poured forth like water,
and which never began without idolatrous sacri-
fices and lying omens ? Their absence from these
things would attract notice; and being noticed,
and questioned, the Christians could not but own
to a wholly different belief to the popular one.

Nor was their belief only different. Christianity,
as it grew more powerful, must have lost its unaggressive character, and claimed to be exclusive
as the sole ground of its existence at all. If God
were God, Jupiter was a devil, and all his worship
devil-worship. No other religion could stand
beside it: if it gained ascendancy, the rest must
be crushed. Now the Romans had admitted all
sorts of foreign religions to an equality with their
own; the mysteries of Osiris and Isis, of the Sun,
and of Dualism, were openly tolerated in Rome;
an emperor would gladly have introduced Christ
to take rank among his country's gods[p]: but
when they saw clearly that either the old religion
or the new must fall, they refused to desert the
old and abide by the new.

This claim of Christianity to be exclusive first
made itself heard in the " Apologies." These
documents, at first no more than fugitive state-
ments of grievances, grew very rapidly into importance, as they were couched in a shape well-
suited to the wants of a necessarily literary body,
till they became a regular series of well-sustained
defences, to which the Church could appeal as

[p] *Euseb.* ii. 2.

D

occasion required. There is a far wider transition
between the matter of the Apologies of Quadratus
and Aristides [q], (A.D. 123.) really no more than a
complaint of "divers evil men," and the attacks
upon pagan absurdities in Justin's first Apology,
written not thirty years after—even than between
this and Tertullian's masterpiece of written ad-
vocacy for the Christian faith, which belongs to
the third century. That the heathen felt the
weight of these recorded arguments is plain from
Celsus' attack on Christianity, probably in answer
to them; a shallow ignorant work, which plainly
shews how unsuccessful Paganism was likely to be
in turning their own weapons against the Christians.
But meanwhile strength, if not right, was on the
pagan side : and the controversy too often ended
in the blood of the Christians, who had thus dared
to be outspoken.

But for all this, the martyrdoms of the second
century were comparatively few. During the
greater part of it the emperors only yielded to
the more and more strongly expressed rancour
of the enemies of the Christians; and thus their
decrees are stamped with a negative character
throughout, prescribing the limits of persecution,
rather than urging it upon their subordinates.
Persecution is hardly the name for this very
reluctant and intermittent warfare. We are able
to give a very exact account of the instructions
for the treatment of Christians given by these

[q] See Fragments of *Quadratus and Aristides*, *Routh's*
'Reliquiæ Sacræ,' (vol. ii. pp. 73, 74.)

emperors to their officers abroad, (tallying sub-
stantially, it is to be presumed, with their own
practice at home); and to compare them with
what we know to have been their actual treatment
of persons accused of Christianity.

(i.) Trajan[r], in his answer to Pliny's letter of
enquiry about the treatment of Christians, re-
commends that they should be let alone, unless
openly accused of Christianity. If brought to
trial, let the nature of the evidence determine the
verdict : the crime is punishable if the evidence is
good, but if it is unsupported, let it be rejected.
Let us see how far Trajan practically acted in the
spirit of this advice. Ignatius, Bishop of Antioch,
had long been notoriously preaching the faith in
his city; in the course of Trajan's reign he is
condemned, brought to Rome, and executed.
But the whole transaction is quite in keeping with
the terms of Trajan's advice to Pliny. Ignatius
had not been touched while unaccused ; when the
emperor was on a visit to Antioch, he was carried
a prisoner, though a willing prisoner[s], before him :
and the evidence must have been too plain and
undoubted to admit of hesitation as to the verdict,
if the terms of the rescript were to be followed;

---

[r] *C. Plin.* epp. x. 98. "Conquirendi non sunt: si de-
ferantur, et arguantur, puniendi sunt: sine auctore vero
propositi libelli nullo crimine locum habere debent."

[s] ἐκουσίως ἤγετο πρὸς Τραϊανόν. ('Martyrium S. Ignatii' from
Jacobson's 'Patres Apostolici.') [The passive voice of ἤγετο
is surely not counteracted by the adverb ἐκουσίως, as 'Clericus'
suggests in his note.]

for all Antioch must have borne witness to his
doctrine and resounded with his preaching.

(ii.) Next, Hadrian answers a like question from
a similarly-situated provincial governor, in a tone
which implies still greater tenderness to the Christians. Reiterating Trajan's instructions, he adds
the following : " Do not punish for Christianity
alone, unless convicted besides of illegality ; and
do not merely reject, but punish false evidence[t]."
What he meant by "illegality," his successor
Antoninus Pius still further defines, saying that
his predecessor forbade punishment for any thing
but plain treason against the Roman sovereignty[u].
We do not hear from history of a single martyr
having suffered in Hadrian's reign, which therefore
has been regarded as a time of unbroken peace to
the Church. But a record has been lately dis-
entombed from the bowels of the earth, which
tells another tale. This is a rudely-carved epitaph,
found in the Catacombs of Rome ; those under-
ground vaults which formed the refuge of the
hunted Christians throughout the early ages, and
which doubtless became more and more a home
to them as persecution thickened. Its simple but
touching language runs as follows[x] : " In the time

---

[t] *Euseb.* iv 9, quoting *Hadrian's* rescript to Minucius Fun-
dacius. εἴ τις οὖν κατηγορεῖ καὶ δείκνυσί τι παρὰ τοὺς νόμους πράτ-
τοντας, οὕτως ὅριζε κατὰ τὴν δύναμιν τοῦ ἁμαρτήματος· ὡς μὰ τὸν
Ἡρακλέα εἴ τις συκοφαντίας χάριν τοῦτο προτείνοι, διαλάμβανε ὑπὲρ τῆς
δεινότητος, καὶ φρόντιζε ὅπως ἂν ἐκδικήσειας.

[u] *Euseb.* iv. 13. οἷς καὶ ἀντέγραψε [πατήρ] μηδὲν ἐνοχλεῖν τοῖς
τοιούτοις, εἰ μὴ φαίνοιντό τι περὶ τὴν Ῥωμαίων ἡγεμονίαν ἐγχειροῦντες.

[x] See *Maitland's* ' Church in the Catacombs,' p. 127.

of the emperor Hadrian, the young Marius, a military officer, (who had lived long enough, when he ended his life in blood for Christ's sake,) at length rested in peace. Erected to the well-deserving in grief and fear[y]." But we may observe, that the execution of Marius was strictly within the letter of Hadrian's rescript. Marius was a military officer, and as such would have the military oaths tendered to him, which as a worshipper of Christ he could not take; he would therefore render himself liable to the punishment for " illegality," or treason against Rome.

(iii.) Antoninus Pius simply confirms[z] the instructions of his predecessor. His conduct, so far as we know, was quite in keeping with the tenor of this confirmation; for we hear of no Christian martyrdoms under his quiet and peaceful reign.

An inscription indeed which has been also found in the Roman Catacombs runs in the following classical and imaginative language: " Alexander is not dead, but lives beyond the stars. . . . . . .

---

[y] The original Latin is as follows: " Tempore Adriani imperatoris Marius adolescens dux militum qui satis vixit dum vitam pro Christo sanguine consunsit in pace tandem quievit benemerentes cum lacrimis et metu posuerunt." [Maitland thinks the word " benemerent*es*" doubtful. May it not be a mistake for benemerent*i*? The last clause would then correspond with the notices of the erection of the epitaphs at the end of many other inscriptions. On p. 131 is a similar omission of the *nominative* to the verb: " benemerent*i* fecit."]

[z] *Euseb.* iv. 26. ταῖς πόλεσι περὶ τοῦ μηδὲν νεωτερίζειν περὶ ἡμῶν ἔγραψεν.

He ended his life in the reign of Antoninus, who,
foreseeing that his good deeds would soon outrun
all hope of payment, returned him evil for good.
...... O luckless times! when, for all our de-
votions and prayers, not even in caverns is safety
possible. ...... He has scarce lived at all, who
has lived in Christian times[a]." What can these
sad times of distress have been? Can the same
emperor who had taken all Christians under his
protection, and who, according to all testimony,
was the mildest ruler that ever sat on a throne,
have merited such a bitter reproach for ingratitude
and cruelty? Surely what is said of the times
agrees much better with the character of those of
the second Antoninus, Marcus Aurelius; who,
during the latter part of his reign, was a stern and

---

[a] *Maitland*, p. 39. The whole of this curious epitaph is
as follows: "Alexander mortuus non est sed vivit super
astra et corpus in hoc tumulo quiescit vitam explevit sub
Antonino imp° *quiubi multum beneficia antevenire prævideret
pro gratia odium reddidit* genua enim flectens vero Deo
sacrificaturus ad supplicia ducitur o tempora infausta quibus
inter sacra et vota ne in cavernis-quidem salvari possimus
quid miserius vita sed quid miserius in morte cum ab amicis
et parentibus sepeliri nequeant tandem in cœlo coruscant
parum vixit qui vixit iv. x. tem." [in Christianis temporibus.
M.]

---

* [Translated as in the text, because of a striking (and it seems
hitherto unperceived) coincidence with a passage of Tacitus, Ann.
iv. 18. "Nam beneficia eo usque læta sunt, dum videntur exsolvi
posse; *ubi multum antevenere, pro gratia odium redditur."* This
cannot surely be an undesigned coincidence; and it is all the more
striking, as it would be written within fifty years after Tacitus'
death.]

relentless persecutor of the Church. It has been conjectured[b], that the alarm of a Marcomannic war (A. D. 166.) first made him persecute the Christians to appease the wrath of the gods: so that this, perhaps, is the most natural time to assign for Alexander's death. The next year saw the martyrdom of Justin, who in his second Apology had predicted his approaching fate; and who was sacrificed by the philosophic Aurelius to the malignity of one Crescens, a Cynic philosopher.

Thus we have seen the century, throughout which the emperors have only reluctantly consented to executions of Christians, end suddenly in blood with the last years of Aurelius' reign. Christians in other countries governed by Rome[c] did not escape the persecution in the capital city; but it was in Rome itself that it must have raged most fiercely. The tone of despair which pervades Alexander's epitaph may be taken to represent the general feelings of Christians at this time. Life was scarce life worth having, when such was the rigour with which Aurelius prosecuted his search, that even the Catacombs were ransacked for victims.

This is the first time that we find the Church attacked on its own merits by Paganism. Before, she had been confounded with Judaism—or, when not confounded, another enemy, not Pagan-

---

[b] *Milman's* ' Early Christianity,' vol. ii. p. 182.

[c] e. g. Polycarp in Smyrna, and the martyrs of Lyons and Vienne.

ism, had been the principal in the persecution. Now first she tasted the bitter cup mixed for her by the conscious opposition of heathen. But even this, bitter as it was, was as nothing to what she was to drain hereafter. The proscription now was set on foot by philosophers, and conducted throughout in a rigorously calm spirit by the philosophic neo-paganism of the day; but the Christians had yet to experience the savage and wanton brutality of persecutors of another stamp, when it came to the last deadly issue, the last struggle for life of the old Polytheism against the new worship.

THIRD
CENTURY.
But for the present a complete lull succeeded the storm. We might almost say, that during the first half of the third century, the vials of wrath ceased their outpouring on the Church. This would be literally true, were it not for the short but savage reign of Maximin, who however treated all religions alike[d] : all the other emperors of the half-century being indifferent, because too insecure in their own seat to be violently opposed to the new religion ; and some even more actively favourable to it. Here then was a long breathing-space between the first and the last persecutions, which the Church ought to have improved to great

---

[d] I omit to notice what is called the persecution of Severus ; because the edict only forbad *proselytism*, not Christian *worship:* and because persecution under it was confined to Africa, and certainly did not extend to Rome. Cf. *Robertson's* " Church History," vol. i. pp. 65, 66.

purpose for strengthening her hands and enlarging the sphere of her work.

But this, her halcyon time as regarded external relations, she unhappily clouded by internal disputes. In her infancy she can hardly be said to have any internal history ; and though she had been growing rapidly for the last century, she had been occupied too exclusively with constant attacks from her exterior foes, to be much concerned about her own inner development. But during this lull between the storms germs of corruption and disunion appear ; questions of faith occasion disputes within her camp. And now too her hierarchy comes into distinct notice. We have hardly heard before of any individual Bishops of Rome. They have been humble men, living in an unmarked dwelling beyond the Tiber*, in the quarter which first received Christianity into Rome : not one that we know of has been conspicuous enough to be called upon to seal his faith with his blood. Now, they suddenly start into individual life ; and grow to exercise that arbitrary power over doctrines as well as discipline, which they are destined to keep for upwards of a thousand years.

Our thoughts naturally turn back to the heretics, as the most likely to disturb the internal peace of the Church during a period of outward quiet. But Orientalism had run itself out in Rome ; the Christians of the West, thoroughly imbued with

* See a note on " Callistus' residence in Trastevere," in *Bunsen's* " Hippolytus and his Age," vol. iv. p. 127.

Christian ideas, no longer doubt about the sole government of the world. All are " Monarchians" in this sense. But they also believed in the Father and the Son ; and it seemed strange that the lips of Monarchians should utter two Divine Names. How could they reconcile the distinct personality of the Two, with the Single Godhead which their Christianity no less bound them to believe ?

Bishop Victor, who headed the orthodox Church in the last ten years of the second century, had met and refuted the two obvious heresies upon this point. On the one hand, he had condemned Theodotus for saying that Christ was a mere man, and that the Father alone was God. But the other solution of the problem was more fanciful and common : at least three heresiarchs held various modifications of the view which has been fatally known to the Church in all ages by the name of Sabellianism ; which said that the Father and Son were not distinct, but operations, energies, or representations of One Monad. Of these, two had been condemned by the same Bishop Victor : Praxeas, who taught himself in Rome ; and Noetus, though his Roman disciple, Epigonus[f].

But Victor was succeeded (A.D. 202.) by Zephyrinus, a weak man, unable to steady himself in the midst of conflicting opinions, and moreover ignorant and venal[g], if we may believe the evidence of

<hr>

[f] *Bunsen's* " Hippolytus," vol. i. pp. 114, 119.

[g] " *Refutatio Hæresium*," p. 285. (published by *E. Miller*, under the title of " *Origenis Philosophumena*," Oxford, 1851,) ἄνδρα ἀγράμματον καὶ ἄπειρον τῶν ἐκκλησιαστικῶν ὅρων ... ὄντα δωρολήπτην καὶ φιλάργυρον, ἔπειθεν.

an adversary.   Callistus, a man of low origin and
disreputable precedents, gained a complete mastery
over him, and swayed him backwards and for-
wards, making him use at different times glaringly
inconsistent language. Sectarian differences ran
high.   The orthodox called the Monarchians
" Patripassians ;" the Monarchians retorted by
the name of " Ditheists," and Callistus, the Pope's
pope, repeated the foul imputation. As long
as he occupied any but the highest place, it was
Callistus' interest that there should be at least
two parties in the Church whom he might play
off upon one another : but as it would embarrass
him if there were more than two, he persuaded
Sabellius, (the third Monarchian, who was just beginning his career,) to coalesce with the Noëtians,
persuading him of the identity of their views[h].

Zephyrinus dying at this juncture, Callistus
stepped into his place (A.D. 218). Having no
further to climb, his policy now was to undo his
former work, and make the Church one. He
threw off Sabellius[i] : and, finding himself unable
to return to the orthodox party after the language
he had used of them, invented a theory of his
own[k], to escape the odious name of Patripassian.
The Father, he said, suffered not *as* the Son, but

[h] R. H. p. 285. ὑπὸ Καλλίστου (Σαβέλλιος) ἀνεσείετο πρὸς τὸ
δόγμα τὸ Κλεομένους ῥαπεῖν, φάσκοντος τὰ ὅμοια φρονεῖν. Cleomenes
was a disciple of Noetus, Bunsen, i. p. 114.

[i] R. H. p. 289. ἀπέωσεν, (qy. excommunicated ?) τὸν Σαβέλλιον.

[k] Ibid. αἰδούμενος τὰ ἀληθῆ λέγειν, διὰ τὸ δημοσίᾳ ἡμῖν ὀνειδίζοντα
εἰπεῖν δίθεοι ἐστέ, ... ἐφεῦρεν αἵρεσιν τοιάνδε.

with the Son, being inseparable from him. This teaching would probably have had more influence and done greater harm to the Church, had it not been accompanied with gross moral perversion. The Pope publicly announced indulgence for sin to all Callistians[1], and openly allowed a system of concubinage even among the clergy. But this was going too far; a revulsion took place towards orthodoxy ; and the whole dispute was soon after drowned in the horrors of Maximin's reign, in which a new Bishop, Pontianus, was the first of the Roman see who was called on to suffer martyrdom for his faith, (A.D. 235.)

The details on this period are borrowed from a lately-discovered work, now generally acknowledged to be by Hippolytus, the contemporary Bishop of Portus, and presbyter of the Roman see. His double position gives us an insight into the constitution of the hierarchy at that time, and shews us the germ of what developed later into the College of Cardinals.

Each of the presbyters at Rome probably had charge of one of the churches of the city. A letter of 251, written by the then Bishop Cornelius, says that there were then forty-six presbyters ; and fifty years later we hear of " more than forty" churches in Rome. During these fifty years then the number had certainly not increased ;—which is strange, considering that the date of the *first* Christian churches in Rome is fixed to only

---

[1] R. H. p. 290. οὐ λογίζεται αὐτῷ ἡ ἁμαρτία, φασὶν, εἰ προσδράμοι τῇ τοῦ Καλλίστου σχολῇ.

twenty years before Cornelius' letter (A.D. 230). The churches were termed " cardines," whence the presbyters who served them were called " cardinales ;" they met regularly to debate on church matters, under the presidency of their bishop. Now a circumstance like that of Hippolytus' being chosen Bishop of Portus when he was already a Roman presbyter, may probably have led to what we afterwards find an undoubted fact :—the introduction of the nine or ten suburbicarian bishops into the council of the cardinals, distinguished by the name of *cardinal-bishops ;* whereas the others were *cardinal-priests.* And when we recollect that it was the former class who, eight centuries after, were invested with the exclusive right of electing the Pope, we shall see the full-blown Roman hierarchy in germ in the third century.

It is tempting to argue from the number of the organized staff to the number of Christians in Rome at this time : but obviously impossible to do it with anything like precision. It would also be an interesting enquiry, if we had materials for conducting it, to trace the gradual increase of the Church from her first few conversions till she had swelled to her third-century proportions : and to find, if possible, indications of the ranks from which she made most converts. But here we are left almost wholly in the dark. We know that St. Paul's labours ranged from the highest to the lowest—from those of Cæsar's household, to the poor runaway slave. We hear of Domitian's

cousin, and a few others of imperial rank in the
course of the three centuries, embracing the
despised religion :—and on the other hand we find,
that the first Christians were sent for a punishment as " *arenarii*" to dig out the sandpits which
formed a network under Rome; and they seem
to have made many converts among that lowest
class. Thus out of the highest and the lowest
rank we can gather some scanty records of proselytism : about the middle class nothing would be
known, were it not that the earth is daily yielding
her treasures, and the Catacombs of Rome are
giving us more and more information about the
class usually unnoticed by history. And yet it is
among these that Christianity must have made
the most way. Revolutions which are destined
to shake a nation do not commonly spring exclusively either from the nobles or the rabble : the
former are in too conspicuous a position for any
change in them to go long unmarked—the latter
exercise too little influence upon the mass of
people. It is the middle rank, receiving from
both extremities, and holding what it receives
tenaciously and noiselessly, which alone is capable
of revolutionizing a state. The yeoman—the
substantial burgher—the mechanic—the retired
scholar—such as these must have formed the
heart and strength of Roman Christianity; though
of this, from the nature of things, we have no
record.

It is of more practical consequence, with regard
to the modern claims of the Papacy, to determine

the degree of recognised authority which the Roman Church possessed over others in the third century. For that Rome had a precedence, and exercised at least a moral influence, can hardly be doubted by any who remember that she was an apostolic Church, the only one in the West; and that she could shew the scenes of the martyrdom of at least two of the Apostles of our Lord[m]. Thus as the depositary of apostolical doctrine, as their elder sister in the faith, other Churches looked up to her, and were willing to follow her precedents. But that there were no pretensions to authority, at least in the *first* century, is plain from the fact, that Clement of Rome (A.D. 91—100), hearing of dissensions in the Church at Corinth, (itself, be it remembered, apostolic, and of at least as early an origin as that of Rome,) had sent the Corinthians a letter[n] " persuading them to peace, and refreshing their faith, and that tradition which they had so lately received from the Apostles." No authority is claimed here—it is the exhortation of an equal, not the imperious demand of a superior.

[m] *Tertull.* 'de præscript. hær.' c. 36. " Si Italiæ adjaces, habes Romam, unde nobis auctoritas præsto est. Ista quam felix ecclesia! cui totam doctrinam apostoli cum sanguine suo profuderunt: ubi Petrus passioni Dominicæ adæquatur: ubi Paulus Joannis exitu coronatur: ubi apostolus Joannes postquam in oleum igneum demersus nihil passus est in insulam relegatur."

[n] *Tertull.* quoted *Euseb.* v. 6. εἰς εἰρήνην συμβιβάζουσα αὐτοὺς, καὶ ἀνανεοῦσα τὴν πίστιν αὐτῶν, καὶ ἣν νεωστὶ ἀπὸ τῶν ἀποστόλων παράδοσιν εἰλήφει.

In the *second* century, however, we find how easily and naturally precedence breeds love of power. The unwarrantable efforts of Bishop Victor (A.D. 170—202), to enforce upon Asia his own practice with reference to the time of Easter, have been already noticed[o]. This dispute between Rome and Asia had been pacified by Gaul[p]; for Irenæus —a third time a 'peacemaker'—had written to Victor a strong letter of remonstrance, which led to his ultimate cession of the point in dispute.

But in the *third* century the utmost claims of Victor are repeated and outdone by Bishop Stephen (A.D. 256); if it is fair to judge from the increased amount of opposition with which they met. Here, as in the former case, Rome had right on her side: but she attempted to enforce that right by tyrannical means, and met with just resistance and signal failure. The difference between the Churches had grown out of what should only have drawn closer the bonds of union—the persecution by Decius. After the long peace of the Church, which had lasted with scarcely an interruption for half a century, it was time that she should be recalled to look to the hole of the pit whence she was digged. Christians had forgotten that they were all one family, all opposed to the world's prevalent belief; and the lesson which should have taught them this, severe and horrible as it was, did but give birth to fresh discords.

Next to Rome, Carthage was the city most exposed to the fury of Decius. The same year

[o] p. 21.   [p] *Euseb.* v. 24.

sent Fabian of Rome to martyrdom and Cyprian of Carthage into retirement. What Rome was to the Italian, Carthage was to the African Churches; till she had grown to rival, if not to equal, Rome in spiritual precedency: and it is curious to see the old strife of the Punic wars played over again under different colours. Their constant intercourse, their community of language, of government, and now of sufferings, could never bind Carthage thoroughly to Rome. The same questions were always rising in both Churches, but always were met with different decisions. It is a Carthaginian that opposes a Roman Bishop in the third century, and the remonstrance comes from an Asiatic.

In 251, with the death of Decius, the persecution came to an end. But so sudden and so severe had it been, that many both in Rome and at Carthage had been shaken in their allegiance to Christ, and had bought their life by the acceptance of " *libelli*," or false certificates of having sacrificed to the heathen gods. Now arose the question as to whether to readmit these libellatics into the Church or not; which both Rome and Carthage had decided in the negative, while the persecution still continued. But when there was no longer any opportunity for them to prove their sincerity by dying for the faith they had denied, Rome and Carthage found themselves at issue as to the amount of penance requisite before readmission; and the two decisions gave rise to schisms in the two Churches. Carthage required rigorous penance as the price of readmission : Rome prescribed milder terms. Yet in Carthage, one Novatus separated from the Church when he was unable to obtain less harsh terms : in Rome, a man of strangely similar name, Novatian, headed a party which enforced greater rigour. Stranger still, Novatus crossed the sea to aid Novatian in designs at Rome, which must have been directly opposed to his own at Carthage.

Novatism at Carthage is soon forgotten— Novatianism at Rome ripens into a confirmed schism. It is when this has lost its vigour, and Novatianist stragglers begin to return to the Church, that a further question arises. How are these schismatics, now more than penitent waverers, to be readmitted ? Rome and Carthage are again at issue. Cyprian decided, that though schismatical baptism was null, a lapse into heresy or schism did not render void an orthodox baptism previously received ; but that in this case the only further ceremony needed to restore a penitent to full Church privileges was imposition of hands. Pope Stephen of Rome held the doctrine which, confirmed by the Council of Arles in 314, is still held by the Church—that baptism was good by whomsoever administered, and therefore that in any case imposition of hands alone was needed. But Stephen went unwarrantable lengths in his efforts to enforce his doctrine. He denounced Cyprian as a false Christ, refused hospitality to his messengers, and broke off communion with the Church of Carthage. On this Firmilian,

Bishop of Cæsarea, and the spokesman of the Churches of Asia Minor, (which themselves had been excommunicated by Stephen for a difference on the same question,) wrote to Cyprian a letter[q], condemning Stephen in the strongest terms for his audacity in arrogating to himself the sole right of dictation on the practice of Christendom. The storm which Stephen had raised from all the Churches was violent indeed ; and the dissension of the third century might have anticipated by eight hundred years the rupture between the East and West, had not the question been fortunately solved by Stephen's death in 257.

The strife between Rome and Carthage was again drowned in blood under Valerian, in a persecution which joined Cyprian and Xystus, Stephen's successor, in the same glorious martyrdom (A.D. 258).

But now the final ordeal of the Church was drawing near. Paganism, which had only inertly and intermittently opposed her before, was now fully awakened to its own impending dissolution. Christianity numbered its tens of thousands even in the capital city, and threatened to outnumber the heathen through all the cities of the empire. It had grown to these alarming proportions, while Paganism had been dallying philosophically with all religious interests : now the authorities felt that their own indifference had fostered it. They saw that there could be no firm standing-point

---

[q] " Firmiliani Epistola ad S. Cyprianum," in *Routh's* " Script. Eccl. Opuscula," (vol. i. p. 217.)

between the many gods of old Rome and the One
God of the Christians; and they hated the latter,
more than they despised the former alternative.
And while terror threw them back upon their old
gods, reviving superstition represented the saving
might of these deserted, but still kind divinities,
in the bright colours of hope. War to the knife,
the extirpation of all the Christians, was now the
only hope of saving the glory of Rome, which
must fall with the fall of her gods.

The persecution in which Galerius, Diocletian,
and Maximin were chief actors, raged through the
whole empire alike for two years, in the East alone
for eight more (A.D. 303—313). It was the last
and deadliest struggle of Polytheism against purity.
The dim conviction that it would be *the last*,
whichever way it resulted—the virulence of the
religion of old Rome, now that it was once more
in possession of the civil arm to wreak its vengeance—and even the reluctance of Diocletian to
take extreme measures until forced into them by
the malignity of his colleague Galerius—all contributed to make this the most searching trial
through which the Church ever had to pass.
Fortunately, trials of the same kind, though
inferior in degree, had lately nerved her to bear
this her last and severest: Decius had found
many, Diocletian found few, to compromise their
faith. Neither age, sex, nor condition exempted
a Christian from agony and death. The leaded
scourges[r], knotted clubs[s], teeth for tearing the

---

[r] " plumbatæ." [s] " scorpiones."

flesh[t], and all the other tortures which malignity could devise, were invented to add to their agony; and when death relieved them, no decent burial was allowed them, but their bones were thrown to the wild beasts, or cast into the Tiber. One martyr alone[u]—probably an unmarked and undistinguished man—was happy enough to be buried in the tomb of his family, with a record which preserves to this day the fact and date of his martyrdom.

But at length the fiery trial came to an end; Diocletian had abdicated, both Galerius and Maximin had died in remorse and torture, and Constantine and Licinius were left alone at the head of the Roman world. The edict of Milan restored Christians to their civil and religious rights; and upon the death of Licinius nine years afterwards, Christianity became established as the religion of the state. At once the Church issued from her temporary depression to enter upon a far wider sphere of power than she had possessed before. Her dark days were over, and centuries of authority and magnificence were now before her. Would that her faith, which up to this time had been refined again and again by affliction, had been

---

[t] " ungulæ."

[u] Lannus is the only martyr who, according to Maitland, has sufficient authentic record of his having suffered under this persecution. His epitaph runs as follows: " Lannus, Xīi martir hic requiescit sub Dioclitiano passus. c. p. s." [et posteris suis]. (*Maitland*, p. 130.)

more proof to the corrupting influences of power
and irresponsibility.

Thus we have found the attempt to trace the
progress and growth of Christianity, through her
days of depression to the opening of her career of
power, to consist mainly of a record of her struggles with three great foes. Of these, we have
seen *Judaism,* perhaps the most bitter of all while
its power lasted, yield the first ;—*Orientalism* ex-
haust its main strength in the second century, yet
still preserve an influence at least on the mode
of thought in the third ;—and *Paganism* retain its
attitude of alternate hostility and indifference, till
it gathers all its strength for the final struggle at
the end of the third century.

It would be more difficult, though perhaps more
practically useful, to gauge the amount and character of the influences which each of the three
permanently left on the Roman Church; for any
permanent impression on this is sure to have
affected in some degree the whole of the Christianity of Western Europe, and to be felt in its
consequences even at the present day.

(i.) After the dispersion of the Jews as a body,
we have seen Judaic principles gradually lose their
hold upon the Roman Church. But though the
distinctive Judaic tenets were sunk thus early, still
to the presence of such a formalizing element may
perhaps be attributable the spirit of *legality,* which
is more and more distinctly traceable in the
Roman Church as it hardens into a systematic

organization, and becomes encrusted with doctrines of late growth and cumbrous rules of discipline. Still the spirit of Christian liberty, which is inherent in the Gospel system as explained by St. Paul, was not extinct within her; an open rupture was always inevitable, but was delayed till the Teutonic kingdoms at last threw off the yoke in the Reformation, and proclaimed their independence of the grievous burdens which the Church of Rome had laid upon their shoulders.

(ii.) Her struggle with Orientalism left its stamp both upon the *doctrine* and upon the *discipline* of the Roman Church; but with different effects upon each. Any cause which made Christians think out and define the doctrines which had only been contained by implication in the early Creeds, must have done invaluable good to the Church, though at the cost of heresies without number. But it is certain that the tendency to asceticism and celibacy, which formed the chief characteristic of the discipline of the mediæval Church, had its origin in the devout tone and lofty aspirations of the Phrygian heretics. This, whatever incidental good it may have done by preserving the religious tone of Europe through the dark ages, cannot now but be regarded as an unmixed evil; at least by those who have protested against the corrupting influences of the Roman monasticism, which is but the systematized form of this tendency.

(iii.) Paganism, with which the Church maintained her struggle the longest, had the greatest effects both for evil and for good upon her character. The good effects are to be sought in the patient constancy, the enduring abnegation of self, with which she went through the ordeal of suffering. With a few exceptions—all jealously noted, yet surely very few in comparison with the many instances of heroic endurance—her sons did not shrink from the danger, nor think it strange concerning the fiery trial which was to try them. Surely some supernatural strength must have been vouchsafed to those who had entered upon the martyr-conflict, to bear them through to the last. But the evil effects were to come when Christianity had apparently gained her triumph over Paganism. Perhaps it was unavoidable that the principle of the defeated superstition should to some extent mingle with the conquering faith; anyhow it is hardly to be doubted that invocation of saints, worshipping of martyrs, and most of the other glosses with which Rome has since overlaid the true faith, are but relics of the religion of the heathen world. May it prove more and more true—as it has to a great extent proved true already—that the Protestant Church, in giving up these spoils of Paganism, has not forfeited an inch of the spirit of true endurance and constancy, with which the Romans went through the furnace of affliction in the three first Christian centuries.

BAXTER, PRINTER, OXFORD.